# JOY RIDE

AN EROTIC ADVENTURE

JADE'S EROTIC ADVENTURES
BOOK 54

VICTORIA RUSH

# VOLUME 54

JADE'S EROTIC ADVENTURES - BOOK 54

# COPYRIGHT

Joy Ride © 2023 Victoria Rush

Cover Design © 2016 PhotoMaras

All Rights Reserved

# ALSO BY VICTORIA RUSH

**Adult Fairytales:**

The Enchanted Forest: An Erotic Fairytale

The Land of Giants: An Erotic Fairytale

The Dragon's Lair: An Erotic Fairytale

Witch's Brew: An Erotic Fairytale

The Mage's Spell: An Erotic Fairytale

The Mermaid Lagoon: An Erotic Fairytale

The Coven: An Erotic Fairytale

Rapunzel: An Erotic Fairytale

The Seven Dwarfs: An Erotic Fairytale

The Land of Mutants: An Erotic Fairytale

The Erotic Temple: A Sexy Fairytale (Coming Soon)

**Erotica Themed Bundles:**

Voyeur: Lesbian Erotica Bundle

Public Affairs: A Lesbian Anthology

Futa Fantasies: The Ladyboy Collection

Threesomes: The Lesbian Collection

Threesomes - Volume 2: The Lesbian Collection

First Time: A Lesbian Anthology

Hedonism: An Erotic Anthology

Switch Hitters: Bisexual Erotica

Taboo Erotica: The Lesbian Series

BDSM: The Lesbian Collection

Party Games: The Erotic Collection

Party Games 2: The Erotic Collection

All Girl 1: Lesbian Erotica Bundle

All Girl 2: Lesbian Erotica Bundle

All Girl 3: Lesbian Erotica Bundle

All Girl 4: Lesbian Erotica Bundle

**Erotic Fairytale Bundles:**

Clover's Fantasy Adventures: Books 1 - 5

Clover's Fantasy Adventures: Books 6 - 10

**Erotic Fantasy:**

Pirate's Bounty: A Time Travel Adventure

Wild West: A Time Travel Adventure

Private Riley: A Time Travel Adventure

Cleopatra's Secret: A Time Travel Adventure

Bounty Hunter 2125: A Time Travel Adventure

Ninja Assassin: A Time Travel Adventure

The 300: A Time Travel Adventure

Arabian Nights: An Erotic Fairytale (coming soon...)

**Steamy Time Travel Bundles:**

Riley's Time Travel Adventures: Books 1 - 5

**Lesbian Erotica:**

The Dinner Party: Lesbian Voyeur Erotica

The Darkroom: Bisexual Voyeur Erotica

Naked Yoga: Lesbian Transgender Erotica

Nude Cruise: Bisexual Voyeur Erotica

Rush Hour: Taboo Public Sex

The Girl Next Door: First Time Lesbian Erotic Romance

Girls' Camp: Lesbian Group Sex

Wet Dream: Ladyboy Fantasy Erotica

The Convent: Taboo Sex with a Nun

Sex Robot: A Dream Sex Machine

The Personal Trainer: Getting Pumped at the Gym

The Dominatrix: BDSM Lesbian Domination

Webcam Chat: Lesbian Online Sex

Paint Me: A Kinky Bodypainting Workshop

The Toy Party: Girls Sharing Sex Toys

The Costume Party: Strapping One On

Swedish Sauna: Lesbian Group Sex

The Therapist: Taboo Lesbian Erotica

Elevator Shaft: Bisexual Threesomes Erotica

Ladyboy: Lesbian Transgender Erotica

Peep Show: Lesbian Voyeur Erotica

The Dare: Public Sex Erotica

Maid Service: Lesbian Threesomes Erotica

The Hitchhiker: First Time Lesbian Erotica

The Housesitter: Spycam Lesbian Erotica

The Spa: Lesbian Group Orgy

Parlor Games: Blindfold Sex Party

The Exchange Student: First Time Lesbian Erotica

The Hostel: Bisexual Group Erotica

The Harem: Lesbian Erotic Romance

The Orient Express: Lesbian Voyeur Erotica

The First Lady: A Forbidden Lesbian Erotic Romance

The Slave: Lesbian BDSM Erotica

The Masseuse: Lesbian Sensuous Erotica

Too Close for Comfort: Lesbian Forbidden Erotica

Naked Twister: A Wild Party Game

Lexi: The Sex App ( Lesbian Fantasy Erotica )

Call Girl: Lesbian Bisexual Threesomes Erotica

Circle Jill: Lesbian Masturbation Workshop

The Viewing Room: Masturbation Voyeur Erotica

Spin the Bottle: A Kinky Party Game

The Hair Salon: Lesbian Voyeur Erotica

Tribadism 1: Girls Only Sex Workshop

Tribadism 2: The Art of Scissoring

Tribadism 3: Threeway Hookups

The Kiss: A Game of Oral Sex

Pledge Week: Sorority Sisters

Carny Games 1: A Wild Sex Party

Carny Games 2: A Kinky Sex Party

Carny Games 3: An Erotic Sex Party

Dreamscape: An Artificial Reality Game

Glory Hole: Guess Who's On the Other Side

Joy Ride: A Late Night Erotic Bus Trip

The Blind Girl: An Erotic Romance(Coming Soon)

**Lesbian Erotica Bundles:**

Jade's Erotic Adventures: Books 1 - 5

Jade's Erotic Adventures: Books 6 - 10

Jade's Erotic Adventures: Books 11 - 15

Jade's Erotic Adventures: Books 16 - 20

Jade's Erotic Adventures: Books 21 - 25

Jade's Erotic Adventures: Books 26 - 30

Jade's Erotic Adventures: Books 31 - 35

Jade's Erotic Adventures: Books 36 - 40

Jade's Erotic Adventures: Books 41 - 45

Jade's Erotic Adventures: Books 46 - 50

Fifty Shades of Jade: Superbundle

**Standalone Stories:**

The Polynesian Girl: A Lesbian EroticRomance

*For the uninhibited...*

# WANT TO AMP UP YOUR SEX LIFE?

*Sign up for my newsletter to receive more free books and other steamy stuff. Discover a hundred different ways to wet your whistle!*

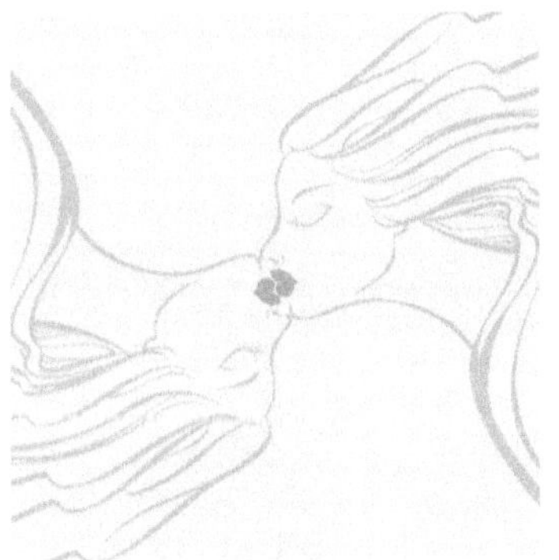

*Victoria Rush Erotica*

**1**

———

It was the worst snowstorm to hit the U.S. Midwest in years. After my return flight to Chicago was finally cleared for takeoff, our pilot informed us mid-flight that O'Hare airport had been closed and that we'd be diverted to Des Moines until the weather cleared. When we landed, I tried desperately to book another flight to the next nearest airport, but everything in the area was snowed in. I had an important business meeting the next day, and getting home late wasn't an option. My only choices were to rent a car or take a coach bus for the long four-hour drive from Iowa to Illinois. But the thought of driving home in the dark on a slippery highway half asleep didn't appeal much to me, so I took a taxi to the local Greyhound station and booked the last coach trip leaving at midnight.

By the time I got on the bus, my phone battery had died and I laid my head on the side glass of my window seat, hoping to catch a few winks before getting ready for my morning meeting. But I was so hopped up on caffeine from drinking coffee all evening that I couldn't sleep. While the other passengers slept quietly around me, I stared out the window, watching the snow-covered fields passing silently beside me while I listened to the quiet rumble of the bus wheels on the interstate highway.

After a half hour or so, I grew bored with nothing to do and, with the cabin pitch dark and everybody sleeping, I slowly unzipped the front of my jeans, slipping my fingers under the waistband of my panties, trying to stimulate my twitching clit. But it was difficult to slide my hand far enough down in my tight-fitting jeans to get sufficient traction, and after glancing over at the girl sitting next to me to make sure she was sound asleep, I quietly reached into my purse for my trusty travel vibrator.

The U-shaped *Tiani* vibrator was the perfect sex toy, small enough to be used discreetly, but large enough to stimulate every part of my erogenous zones. The fat, bulbous end nested perfectly inside my pussy to stimulate my G-spot, while the flat, curved end pressed against my clit, providing dual stimulation to generate the most amazing blended orgasms. And the best part was that it came with a separate controller that I could use to stimulate myself remotely while I concentrated on the sensation of the device humming inside me.

Keeping one eye on the girl sleeping next to me, I slowly stuffed the vibrator down the front of my pants, gently slipping the fat end into my dripping pussy. After I positioned the device against the underside of my vulva, I leaned my head back against the seat cushion and closed my eyes, gently tapping the buttons on the remote control to select my favorite pulse pattern. Thank heavens I'd had the presence of mind to recharge the battery in my hotel room before I left for the airport. With almost three hours of runtime at normal speed, I hoped it would last long enough to keep me entertained for the rest of my trip.

I clicked the mode button until I felt the alternating pulse pattern that I used to edge for long periods, slowly turning the flywheel on the remote until I reached a comfortable buzz on my tingling button. While I concentrated on the vibrations radiating inside my throbbing pussy, I slowly spread my knees apart, grazing the girl's thigh resting next me. She stirred for a moment, then she snorted softly before turning her head in the other direction, resting her arms over her rising and falling chest.

Satisfied that she was still asleep, I felt confident enough to turn the vibration speed up until it was humming loudly inside me. Thankfully, the sound of the bus wheels on the wet highway muffled the sound of the vibrator, and as my pleasure began to grow, I spread my legs apart once again, twisting the flywheel until the device was vibrating hard inside me. The feeling of the fat tip rubbing against my G-spot while the thin end simultaneously buzzed against my tingling gland was impossible to resist, and within a few minutes I was gyrating my hips as I tried to stifle groans.

When I reached the tipping point and couldn't hold back the floodgates any longer, I grunted loudly while I gushed into my panties, jerking softly in my seat while I enjoyed a long, luxurious climax in the privacy of my darkened seat. After my contractions finally began to ebb, I turned the vibrations off on my controller, savoring the exquisite feeling of the two-pronged vibrator resting quietly inside me.

"That was *hot!*" my seatmate suddenly said, nudging me gently with her elbow.

"What?" I said, horrified that I'd awoken her with my squirming and moaning and been discovered in the act.

"Don't worry," the girl said, smiling at me while she glanced down at my wet crotch. "Your secret is safe with me.

But I'm intrigued what you're using to stimulate yourself. I can hear the sound of a vibrator, but it appears to be perfectly disguised."

"It's a special U-shaped one that fits snugly against your pussy," I nodded, becoming newly aroused by her interest in my vibrator. "One side goes inside to stimulate your G-spot while the other end stimulates your clit."

"No way!" the girl said, flaring her eyes open in excitement. "Can I give it a try? I mean, that is, if you're finished stimulating yourself..."

**2**

---

"**I** was planning on using it to keep myself amused for the remainder of the trip," I said. "But watching *you* using it will be almost as much fun. Let me just take a minute to clean it off for you..."

I pulled the device out of my pants and reached into my purse for a wet-wipe, but the girl grabbed my hand holding the vibrator, rubbing her thumb softly over the slippery fat end.

"There's no need," she smiled. "It's already nicely lubricated and I want to feel your juices mingling with mine. How do I turn it on?"

"You control it using this device," I said, showing her the remote control. "These buttons control the pulse pattern and this little wheel controls the level of the intensity–"

"Can you control it *for* me?" the girl said. "It will be more fun with you stimulating me, and that way I can concentrate on the feelings inside me."

"My feelings exactly," I nodded, releasing my grip on the vibrator as she pulled it toward her.

She turned it around in her hands for a few seconds

while she examined it, then she slowly unzipped her pants, trying to stuff it under her tight panties.

"How did you ever manage to get this thing *inside* you?" she said, pinching her eyebrows together in frustration.

"I've had a little extra *practice*," I chuckled. "You might need to loosen your pants a bit more."

The girl paused as she peered across the aisle at the passengers sleeping in the adjacent rows, then she nodded her head, wiggling her butt while she shimmied her jeans down over her knees. Then she pulled the waistband of her panties open and stuffed the fat end of the vibrator over her slit, slowly slipping it inside her.

"Unghh," she groaned when she felt the thick bulb pressing against her G-spot.

"Press it up against your vulva until you feel the other end resting over your clit," I nodded, feeling my pussy throbbing in sympathy with her. "Can you feel it squeezing you from both sides?"

"Yes," she panted, writhing in her seat. "It feels heavenly. I could probably come just by moving my hips all by myself–"

"Maybe," I smiled, picking up the remote control and tapping the pulse button. "But it's a lot more fun when you play with the settings."

I tapped the button once, and the vibrator gently began throbbing about a second apart.

*"Nnngg,"* the girl groaned, spreading her legs further apart.

"Better?" I said.

"Better," she nodded. "What else does this thing do?"

"I'm glad you asked," I said, turning the flywheel while I increased the intensity of the pulse signal.

"Oh God–" she panted, thumping her head against her headrest, shaking the seat roughly.

"Try not to move so much," I said, placing my finger over her lips. "You'll wake the rest of the passengers. We don't want to get arrested by the cops when we arrive in Chicago."

"Mmm," she purred, wrapping her lips around my digit and sucking it into her mouth. "Give me more. I want you to watch me come while I'm looking at you."

"Yes," I smiled, pressing my free hand down the front of her panties to feel the vibrator shaking against her wet pussy. Then I tapped the pulse button two more times until it began to vibrate steadily, slowly turning the wheel until the device hummed loudly inside her.

"Fuck, that feels good," the girl said, spreading her knees far apart while I tickled the sides of her dripping labia. "I'm going to come if you keep doing that–"

"That's the idea," I said, pulling my finger out of her mouth and slipping my hand under her blouse while pinching one of her nipples with two fingers.

"Yes," she panted, raising her hips off her chair as she approached climax. "Squeeze my nipples. I'm going to come so hard–"

Suddenly, she let out a low guttural groan while she pressed her pussy against my hand, and I pulled my other hand out from under her blouse and slapped it over her mouth to muffle her squeals of delight while she jerked her hips against my hand as she stared at me with glassy eyes.

"Yes, baby," I purred, gazing at her while she jerked in her chair, dripping her juices out of her throbbing hole and down the insides of her legs.

"That was *insane!*" she said, slumping into her seat after she came down from her climax. "I don't know what I enjoyed more–the danger of being discovered by the other passengers while I got off, or your feeling me up while I came quietly beside them."

"It wasn't so *quiet*," I chuckled, caressing the inside of her dripping thighs while I turned off the vibrator controls.

"Sorry," the girl said. "It was kind of impossible to control myself. That was the sexiest thing I've ever done. I don't know how I'll ever be able to top that experience–"

"I dunno," I smiled. "I was thinking of something *else* we could do that would take this to an entirely new level..."

"I can't imagine what that might be," the girl said. "But at this point, I'm game for anything. I'm so horny, I could fuck a door handle right now."

"I was thinking of something a little more *animated*," I said, pulling the vibrator out of her pussy and flexing the two ends apart. "But perhaps we should introduce ourselves before going any further. After all, it looks like we're going to be getting a lot closer over the next couple of hours..."

"Joy," the girl said, holding out her hand next to me.

"Jade," I said, gripping her hand with my slippery fingers. "You better get ready, because we're about to have one hell of a joy ride..."

**3**

———

"What exactly did you have in mind?" Joy said while she watched me pull off my pants and underwear in the darkened cabin.

"If you thought it was fun to use this thing by yourself, wait until you try it in tandem with another girl," I smiled.

"You mean, attached *together*?" Joy said, flaring her eyes.

"Is there any other way?" I said, slipping the fat end of the vibrator inside my pussy.

"How exactly are you planning to do this?" she said, peering at me with a wrinkled brow. "There's not much room in this cramped seat row..."

"There's enough room for you to sit on top of me," I nodded. "Just bend your knees while you squat down overtop of me, and I'll take care of the rest."

Joy turned her head while she glanced at the sleeping passengers sitting on the other side of the aisle, then she pulled her jeans down the rest of the way and slipped off her panties, carefully crawling on top of me to make the minimum amount of noise. When I felt her pubic hair caressing the bottom of my shaved mound, I slipped the thin end inside her dripping slit, and she rested her hips against my flared legs, pressing the curved connector hard against my throbbing nub.

*"Damn,"* Joy panted, kissing me hard on my lips. "That *does* feel a lot better!"

"It'll feel even better when I turn the device on," I grinned, slipping my tongue inside her mouth while I tapped the pulse button on the remote control.

The Tiani vibrator began throbbing inside both of our pussies and Joy moaned softly into my mouth, writhing her hips gently against mine. I unbuttoned the top buttons of her blouse and slipped my hands under her bra, squeezing her tits while I ground my pussy against hers. The feeling of the joined connector rubbing against my gland magnified the sensation of the device throbbing inside our pussies, and I pulled her ass harder toward me, pressing the two ends of the device harder against our respective G-spots.

"Oh my God," Joy grunted, rocking her hips up and down over my mound to rub our clits together. "You weren't kidding, this is a million times better when we do it together."

"Yeah," I said, glancing through the seat cushions at the passengers sleeping in the forward row. "But try to keep your movement to a minimum. We don't want to wake the passengers in the other rows. Let the vibrator do most of the work, and just enjoy the sensation."

I twisted the flywheel on the remote a few degrees further forward, and the vibrator began buzzing harder, creating a blended rumble radiating over our connected hips.

"That's easy for *you* to say," Joy groaned, squeezing the

sides of my hips with her thighs as her pleasure began to mount. "You've got the backrest to support you while I'm pinning you to the seat. It's not so simple for me to remain still while this thing is vibrating inside me."

"I see your point," I teased. "Do you want me to turn the speed down so you can control yourself more easily?"

"*Fuck* no," Joy rasped, tilting her hips harder against mine. "This feels way too good just the way it is. Your bare pussy feels delicious next to mine."

"I like your soft hairs," I nodded, dancing my tongue inside her mouth while she squirmed her hips overtop of mine. "It's adding an extra degree of stimulation to the experience."

"Your bare pussy is driving me crazy," Joy nodded. "I want to suck your cunny so bad..."

"If you're a good girl and don't wake up the rest of the passengers," I smiled, "that could be arranged. Are you getting close?"

"Yes," she grunted, gyrating her hips more roughly against mine. "Can you turn it up any faster?"

"I think there's a bit more power on reserve," I nodded, twisting the flywheel to the maximum setting.

Suddenly, the Tiani began buzzing hard between our joined hips, and Joy grunted loudly, shaking my seat forcefully as she jerked her body against me. I noticed the head of one of the passengers sitting in front of me twist to the side, and I tapped the pulse button, temporarily turning off the vibrator.

"What are you doing?" Joy said, pulling her head back and looking at me with a flushed face. "I was almost there. I just needed a few more seconds..."

"We're waking up the rest of the cabin," I said, placing

my finger over her lips again to quell her excitement. "Let's just rest for a moment until everybody goes back to sleep."

"At this point, I don't even care," Joy panted. "Why don't we give them a little show? It'll probably be the most excitement they've had all day."

"I just don't want anybody telling the *driver*," I nodded. "I'm not sure everybody would be onboard with the idea of an impromptu sex show. There are probably rules against this sort of thing–"

"We're a long way from the front of the bus," Joy grunted. "Just turn the vibrator on halfway, and I promise to be quieter. It won't take me long to finish now."

"Okay," I said, noticing the rest of the passengers appearing to rest quietly in their seats with their eyes closed. "But you better kiss me, just to be safe. I don't trust you squealing too loudly when you come again."

"Mmm," Joy moaned, pressing her lips against mine. "My pleasure."

"Mine too," I smiled, tapping the remote control and twisting the flywheel forward.

It didn't take long for our pleasure to ramp up to the tipping point with our hips tightly connected and the vibrator throbbing against our G-spots as we mashed our clits together, writhing in delicious agony. Suddenly Joy wrapped her arms around my shoulders, pulling my body hard against hers while her hips began jerking wildly in my lap. When I felt her coming, I couldn't hold back my climax any longer, and as I felt the pressure releasing, I gushed my juices all over her pussy, squirting jets of fluid between our joined abdomens. Joy's eyes flared open when she felt me spurting over her perineum, and she grunted into my mouth while I held her head tightly against my face to muffle her screams.

But by the time we finished climaxing in our shaking seat, I turned around to notice half of the bus had awoken and were squinting in the darkness at the two strange women sitting on top of each other, holding on to each other like they'd just been cast adrift in a rocking lifeboat.

**4**

———————

"Holy *shit*," the girl sitting on the opposite side of the aisle said, rubbing her crotch while she stared at the two of us sitting on each other's laps. "Can *I* get some of that? That was the hottest thing I've seen in a long time!"

"Possibly," I smiled, pulling the dripping Tiani vibrator out of my pussy while Joy slumped back in her seat, pulling up her pants. "Did you want to try out my special *toy*, or were you thinking of something a little more interactive?"

"What *is* that thing exactly?" the girl said, darting her eyes between the rubbernecking passengers.

"It's a vibrator," I whispered, holding the gleaming device up in the moonlight shining through my window.

"That doesn't look like any vibrator *I've* seen before," the girl said.

"Here," I said, tossing the cum-soaked device across the aisle, where the girl caught it unsteadily with two hands.

I tapped the pulse button on the remote control and slid the wheel partway forward. The girl jerked her hands in surprise when she felt the two ends of the Tiani vibrating, then she twisted her head toward me, peering at me with a puzzled expression.

"How does it work?" she said, turning the U-shaped device around slowly in her hands. "Which end goes *inside*?"

"Technically, either one," I smiled. "But the fat end provides better stimulation for your G-spot, while the thin end stimulates your clit on the outside."

"May I–?" the girl said, flexing the two ends of the vibrator inquisitively.

"Knock yourself out," I nodded, turning to see if anyone was still watching.

The girl peered around her and when she was satisfied no one else was paying attention, she slowly removed her pants and underwear, laying them on the empty aisle seat beside her. Then she turned around, resting her back against the side window while spreading her legs apart for us to see as she angled the fat tip of the Tiani toward her glistening slit.

"Oh my God," Joy rasped, pulling her pants back down over her hips and sliding her fingers under her drenched panties. "Just when I thought it couldn't get any hotter in here."

"Yeah," I said, not even bothering to put my clothes back on while I slid my left hand over my dripping slit as I grasped the remote control in my other hand. "It looks like we might have started a little chain reaction…"

"Something tells me we're going to get the rest of the bus in on the action before this trip is finished," Joy chuckled, noticing two men sitting on the back bench behind our row unzipping their pants and pulling out their hard-ons while they squinted through the narrow opening in the other girl's seatback.

"That's fine with me," I smiled, shoving two fingers inside

my hole while I watched the two men stroking their cocks openly beside one another.

"Unghh," the girl in the opposite row groaned when she slipped the thick end of the vibrator into her opening.

"You *like*?" I grinned, tapping the button on the controller to increase the frequency of the pulse pattern on the G-spot end.

"Fuck yes," the girl groaned, pressing the other end against her clitoris while she began to rock her hips slowly.

"How about *this*?" I said, tapping the second button to activate the clitoral end of the vibrator.

"Oh *fuck*," she nodded, feeling the other tip buzzing against her gland. "Don't stop. This thing is amazing!"

"It's pretty cool," I nodded, noticing Joy's fingers sliding inside her tunnel while she watched the other girl. "Comes in handy on boring nights when there's nothing to do."

I leaned over and slipped my free hand under Joy's blouse and unclasped her bra, squeezing one of her breasts while I pinched her nipple.

"You guys are so hot," the girl across the aisle said, gaping her mouth open while she watched the two of us jilling ourselves as we stared at her glistening pussy, clamped by the two vibrating tips of the Tiani vibrator.

"Maybe we can figure out how to do a *three-way* if we don't wake up the rest of the bus by the time you're finished," I grinned, darting my eyes between Joy's strumming fingers and the other girl writhing her hips while a deep flush began to rise up over her neck.

"Fuck, yes," the girl grunted, spreading her legs further apart as she slowly raised her hips off her seat, nudging ever-closer toward climax. "I have a feeling we won't need this thing if there's three of us involved. I want to *taste* your pussies next time..."

"I think there might be enough room on your side to accommodate *all* of us," I nodded. "I'm ready to come over anytime–"

"Just one more second," the girl panted, arching her hips higher in the air as her mouth gaped open in mounting pleasure. "I want to see what it feels like to come with this thing inside me. Oh God, here it comes. *Nngahhh!*"

When Joy and I saw the other girl's hips shaking uncontrollably while she held them raised above her seat with her thighs spread far apart, both of us tumbled over the edge together, shaking in our seats while we pressed our knees tightly together over our embedded hands, trying not to add to the loud groans of the girl opposite our aisle. When all of us had finally recovered from our orgasms, we heard the grunting of the two men behind us, and we glanced over just in time to see them squirting their loads high over their heads while they leaned forward, trying to get a better view of three of us through the cracks in our chairs.

"Mmm," I said, nodding approvingly at their twitching cocks in their tight fists. "Did you guys enjoy that show as much as we did?"

"Fuck, yes," the first one said, nodding toward his friend. "Though we'd enjoy it a whole lot *more* if the three of you joined us back here. There's plenty of room for all of us to stretch out."

"I don't know," I smiled, peering at my two new girlfriends. "I think it would be almost as much fun watching the two of you making out first."

"You mean *touching* each other?" the other guy said, pinching his eyebrows together in dismay. "But we're not gay–"

"You just jerked off side-by-side," I chuckled. "If that's not gay, I don't know what is."

"What exactly do you want us to do?" the first guy said, peering at his friend awkwardly.

"I don't know," I grinned. "Why don't you surprise us? If you put on a good enough show, maybe we'll join you for the next round. That is, if you think you've got enough juice left in the tank..."

The two men peered at one another for a moment, then their flopping dicks began to rise again between their legs as they reached out tentatively to grasp each other's tools...

**5**

———

While the two men began to stroke each other's cocks, Joy, the other girl and I turned around in our seats, peering through the cracks in the chairs while we gently played with our pussies. The men seemed reluctant to go much further, even though the looks on their faces belied the pleasure they were feeling as they stimulated themselves.

"Come on," I teased. "You can do better than that. At least take off your *pants* so we can see all of your equipment. It'll be a lot more fun if you can play with each other's *balls* at the same time."

The two men peered at one another, then they glanced through the holes in the seatbacks, noticing the three of us smiling back at them, then they pulled down their pants and boxers, throwing them on the seat next to them.

"That's better," I nodded, noticing their tight balls resting against the base of their bobbing hard-ons. "Now play with each other's balls while you stroke your partner's dick."

"Unghh," the first man groaned when his friend cupped

his sack and squeezed his testicles while he twisted his hand over his flaring glans.

"Mmm," I hummed, glancing over at the two girls. "It's nice to watch two guys jerking off for a change, isn't it ladies? They know exactly what they like, because they've had a lot of practice."

"Yes," Joy nodded, circling her clit with the two fingers of her right hand while she watched the men stroking one another. "I bet they know how to *suck* each other's cocks better than women too. I'd love to see them go down on each other–"

"What do you say, boys?" I said. "Are you ready to take it to the next level?"

"Umm..." the first guy said, making an uncomfortable face while he peered at his friend.

"Come on," I goaded them. "You know you want it. Show us girls how you like it, and maybe we'll follow your lead when you're done."

"You mean you want us to come in each other's *mouths*?" the second guy said, scrunching his face up into a disgusted expression.

"Why not?" I smiled. "You always expect us girls to swallow your cum. It's high time you learned what it tastes like. But don't worry, you'll be much too busy enjoying the feeling of your partner sucking your dick to barely notice when the other guy comes."

"Okay," the second guy said, a drop of precum excitedly spilling out of the slit in his crown. "But how will we do it at the same time?"

"Why don't one of you lie down on the bench while the other one sixty-nines him from above?" I said. "That way, we girls can watch all the action, and you can have full access to your partner's entire perineum. Apparently, that's the favorite spot for gays to play with each other."

"But we're not gay–" the second man protested.

"Says the guy who's got his hand wrapped around his friend's dick," I chuckled. "Give it a try. You can close your eyes if it makes you feel any better. I'm pretty sure one mouth feels as good as any other, once you get into it. We won't tell anyone, I promise."

The first man cocked his head and shrugged his shoulders, indicating he was game if his partner was, then they quickly assumed the sixty-nine position, staring at each other's upturned hard-ons while rivulets of precum streamed down the sides of their bobbing erections.

"Go ahead," I said, sticking my fingers in my pussy, becoming increasingly turned on by the two straight guys' growing sexual attraction. "Taste it, it won't kill you."

They stuck their tongues out and flicked the tip over their flaring heads, causing them to groan and spit out another drop of cum.

"See, it's not so bad, is it?" I smiled, sinking my fingers knuckle-deep in my hole.

"Uhhn," the two men nodded, circling their tongues around the base of each other's glans while they tilted their hips higher toward their partner's faces.

"Fuck, that's hot," Joy hissed, tribbing her clit harder as her moistening pussy began to slurp and smack from her rapid jilling action.

"They seem to like that spot," the other girl said, staring at the two men licking each other's tools with wide eyes while she massaged her glistening pussy.

"I told you," I nodded. "Only a guy really knows how to give another guy a proper blow job. Go ahead, suck your partner's helmet into your mouth and show us how you *really* like it."

The two men lowered their heads, engulfing the entire tip into their mouths, moaning louder while they humped their dicks against their partner's faces.

"Mmmft," the first one groaned, squeezing the shaft of his friend's dick and beginning to stroke it up and down.

"Hufft," the second one hissed, cupping the balls of his friend and strumming his fingers under the base of his shaft.

"Yes," I grunted, starting to feel the familiar pangs of an impending orgasm building inside me once again while I watched the two men playing with each other's equipment. "Work the entire area. Show us how you like it."

As the two men began grunting harder, they lowered their heads further down the other's pole while they stroked the shaft rhythmically and squeezed their partner's balls.

"Yes," I groaned, watching them suck each other with increased urgency. "I want to watch you come in each other's mouths. This is crazy-hot."

"Mmmh-nnghh," the men groaned together, rolling their hips in unison while their partner sucked the other's dick like he hadn't eaten in a week.

"So they *do* like to take as much of their cocks down their throats as possible," Joy smiled, gaping her mouth open while she mimicked the technique of each man.

"So much for having an aversion to *touching* each other," the other girl chuckled, watching the men lowering their mouths all the way down to the base of their partner's dripping dick, relaxing their throat muscles while they took the entire organ into their cavity.

"Let it rip, boys," I nodded. "You'll barely even notice

when the other one comes now. Swallow his spunk while you ram your dick down his gullet..."

*"Uhn, uhn, uhn,"* both men huffed while their faces became increasing flushed from their mounting pleasure.

Suddenly, they grunted loudly as they lifted their respective hips off the bench seat, shoving their cocks as far into each other's mouths as they could while they emptied their seed down the other's throat. I watched with excitement while their perineums pulsed in rhythmic contractions as their prostates contracted and spurted their loads into their mouths.

"Do you *see* that?" I said to the other girls, pointing toward their pulsing anuses.

"Fuck, yeah," Joy hissed, jerking her hips in sympathy with the men while she came hard watching them come in each other's mouths.

"I almost wish I was a *man* right now," the other girl nodded, flapping her knees together while she climaxed along with them. "I've never seen anything like that before."

"I have a feeling there's a lot more where that came from," I grinned, feeling my own pussy clamping down on my fingers while I gushed my juices over my hand. "I can't wait to see what the *five* of us can do once we get together."

**6**

———

"Ahhh," the men groaned happily when they finally lifted their heads off one another's erections, slumping back in their seats as their dicks dribbled over their abdomens.

"*Still* think it's a sin to suck another man's cock?" I said to the two guys as they lay back on their seat rests with satisfied grins on their faces.

"I suppose not," the first man grinned sheepishly, glancing sideways at his friend's still raging hard-on.

"*Definitely* not," the second man laughed, peering down at his bobbing erection.

"Don't lose that thought," I nodded, glancing at the other girls. "Because I think we might be able to make it even *more* interesting if you let us join you in the next round."

"But there's only *two* of them and three of us," Joy said, peering at me with a wrinkled brow. "How are we going to make that work?"

"I was thinking about that the entire time they were sucking each other's dicks," I nodded. "They may only have two cocks, but they also have two *mouths*. I've got an entirely *different* idea how we can stimulate each other next time around."

"What did you have in mind?" the first man said, glancing down at his flagging organ. "I'm not sure I'm going to be hard enough to put it inside one of your pussies..."

"Let me worry about that," I smiled, motioning for the other girls to join them on the back row. "This time, I want you to lie down facing each other, balls-to-balls. Then the two girls can sit on your faces, facing one another while you eat their pussies."

"What about our *dicks*?" the second guy said. "How are you going to satisfy yourself if we're not hard anymore?"

"I've got an idea how I can get you back in the game," I smiled, joining the other girls in the back row and kneeling on the floor in front of the two men's cocks as they assumed the position.

"Mmm," I smiled, picking up their sagging organs and pressing them together, slowly stroking my hands over their slippery shafts coated with cum.

"Mhhh," the first guy groaned, tilting his head up to watch me stroking their two cocks together as they slowly humped their hips in unison.

"Nnghh," the second guy rasped, enjoying the feeling of me jerking their joined cocks.

"*Shit*, that's hot," Joy said, kneeling over the first guy's head and lowering her twitching clit onto his face while she watched me working their fattening tools.

"Fuck, yes," the other girl said, joining Joy on the other side and mashing her pussy against the second man's lips. "This is another first for me."

"It's called *frotting*," I nodded, noticing both of the men's cocks quickly growing back to full attention as they humped their hips together while I encircled their two erections with both hands. "It's another way gays like to have sex with each other..."

"I told you, we're not ga–" the first man said before Joy pressed her pussy hard over his mouth, squeezing her thighs tightly against his face.

"Yeah, yeah," she said, rolling her eyes. "Your *cocks* seem to have a mind of their own. Just shut up and suck my pussy while I watch Jade play with your tools."

"It's a shame you can't get a piece of that," the other girl said, rocking her hips against the second guy's face while her chest began to flush in excitement. "They're too busy *fucking* each other for you to get in on the action."

"What makes you think I can't get in on the action?" I grinned, standing up and turning around while I pointed my butt over their joined dicks.

"You mean–?" Joy said, widening her eyes as I positioned my dripping pussy over their flaring organs.

"Yup," I nodded, reaching one hand between my legs and pulling their tips toward my opening. "I've got a *different* kind of DP in mind for these two guys."

"No fair!" the second girl said, leaning forward as she slid the palms of her hands down the flexing abdomen of her partner while he lifted his hips up to meet my dripping hole. "You had this planned all along! You get both cocks at the same time while we're relegated to only using their *mouths*."

"I don't see you complaining *too* much," I smiled, feeling the tips of the men's cocks spreading me apart as their joined poles began to enter my tight tunnel. "Shut up and enjoy the show while you teach the guys how to eat your pussies. If they've still got anything left in the tank after this latest round, maybe we can switch positions and enjoy the show from another angle."

"Oh my God," Joy groaned, leaning forward at the same time while the two girls played with my tits as I lowered myself down over the two men's throbbing organs. "I wouldn't have believed this was *possible* if I hadn't seen it firsthand."

'Maybe you'll be the *second* pair of hands the next time around," I nodded, lowering myself all the way over their throbbing cocks while I flexed my legs and bobbed up and down over their thick organs.

"Fuck *that*," Joy hissed. "I'm going to fuck their cocks with my *pussy* if I get the next chance."

"You hear that, boys?" I chuckled, listening to the two men groaning underneath me while they slapped their hips against my dripping pussy, gnashing their balls together. "They're lining up to get a piece of you. Did you ever think it could be this much fun to rub your dicks together?"

"Shit no," the first man grunted while catching a breath under Joy's gyrating hips.

"Fuck, I'm going to come again," the second guy shuddered as he dug his fingertips into the sides of the seat cushion.

"Yes, baby," I growled, feeling my orgasm approaching like a freight train. "Let me feel both of you pulsing inside me while you come together. I'm just about ready..."

"Oh *fuck*," the first man rasped as he flexed his legs opposite his friend's shoulders, curling his toes downward while his balls tightened and he began pulsing inside me.

"Holy shit, Joe," his friend grunted, tightening his grip on the seat cushion until his knuckles began to turn white. "I can feel your dick throbbing against mine. I'm going to come with you..."

When I felt both of their cocks pulsing inside me, my pussy tented over their spurting dicks, then I clamped down hard while I went into paroxysms of pleasure, jerking my hips wildly over their joined poles as I gushed my juices over their elevated balls. When the two girls saw me squirting over their abdomens, they slumped their bodies over my shaking shoulders, wrapping their arms around me while all five of us groaned in delirious ecstasy.

It wasn't until all of us had recovered from our synchronized orgasms that I noticed a lineup had formed in the aisle leading up to the rear bench, with men and women of all ages peering over each other shoulders, eager to join in on the kinky sideshow of the randy passengers at the back of the bus.

"Have you got room for a few more?" a handsome college student said, unzipping his bulging fly.

"And perhaps a couple more *women*?" two cute girls said, holding each other's hands.

"The more the merrier," I nodded, glancing toward the front of the cabin and noticing the driver peering into his rear-view mirror, grinning like a Cheshire Cat while he steered the bus with one unsteady hand.

**7**

———

"How are we going to pull *this* one off?" Joy said, squinting at me with a confused expression. "Now there's three cocks and five pussies. And there's not enough room for anyone else to lie down back here–"

"Well, *actually*," one of the new girls said, unzipping the front of her jeans and pulling out an impressively large dick. "You've got *four* cocks to work with, so it's pretty evenly balanced out now..."

"Hmm," I smiled, peering at the rest of my friends and glancing at the row of seat cushions lined up against the back wall. "I think we all might be able to fit if we sit side-by-side, boy/girl, boy girl. What's your name, sweetheart?"

"Samantha," the pretty trans girls said.

"I'm Abigail," her friend smiled.

"My name's Jade," I nodded, and this is Joy and–"

"Lisa," the other girl said.

"Joe," the first man said, staring at Samantha's hardening tool.

"Owen," his friend said, unable to take his eyes off Samantha's dripping hard-on.

"Jake," the new guy said, equally smitten by the pretty ladyboy's equipment.

"Now that we're properly introduced," I grinned. "Why doesn't Sam sit in the middle of the seat since everybody already seems distracted by her beautiful cock, while the rest of us sit hip-to-hip next to her, playing with each other while we take in all the action?"

Samantha quickly pulled off her jeans and sat down in the center of the console with her big dick pointing straight up, then Abigail and I staked out positions flanking each side of her, with the rest of the group alternating boy-girl as I had instructed.

"Four hard cocks," Joy nodded approvingly, licking her lips while her eyes darted up and down the row of upturned erections.

"And four beautiful pussies," Jake said, sitting next to her.

"Well, what are we waiting for?" I grinned. "Let's get the party started!"

Abigail and I grabbed Samantha's cock hand-over-hand, stroking her instrument up and down while she rested her head against the backrest and spread her legs further apart. Beyond her thick, beautiful cock, she looked just like any other woman, with full, bouncy tits, hourglass-shaped hips, and rosebud lips panting below her long, flappy eyelashes. While I stroked her cock with one hand, I caressed her breasts with the other, and she leaned over to kiss me as she moaned into my mouth.

"You're beautiful," I mumbled while we lashed our tongues together.

"So are you," she said, reaching her hand between my legs and inserting two fingers inside my sopping pussy.

While she fingered me with her digits, she rolled her thumb expertly over my clit as my juices began to roll over her hand.

"You seem to know your way around a woman's pussy pretty well for a girl with a *cock*," I groaned.

"And you squirt your juices just like a *man*," she grinned, watching my lubrication running down the insides of my thighs.

"I guess we both have our hidden talents," I smiled, feeling her precum dribbling down the side of her shaft while I worked the head of her dick and her friend played with her balls.

Samantha glanced beside her, watching the others stroking and fingering each other as their eyes darted up and down the line, taking in the erotic show.

"It looks like everybody else is rapidly getting in the mood," she smiled.

"I think you're the *main* attraction," I chuckled, noticing everyone's eyes returning to the ladyboy's large phallus while Abby and I stroked her pole harder.

"It's only because I'm in the middle," she grunted as her balls beginning to tighten around the base of her cock.

"Oh, I suspect it's for more reasons than just *that*," I grinned, peering at her pretty face as her cheeks began to flush in rising pleasure. "Why don't you give them something to remember by coming all over your pretty tits while Abby and I hold your cock?"

"Mmm, fuck yes," Samantha hummed, squeezing her buttocks and lifting her hips a few inches off her seat. "I can feel it coming..."

Suddenly, she spurted a series of thick ropes out of her

flaring slit, spraying her spunk all over her bouncing breasts while the rest of the group grunted loudly, unable to hold back their own rising pleasure any longer, shaking their bodies in a series of coordinated convulsions as I spread my legs and jetted my juices over the floor of the aisle.

When I recovered from my orgasm, I glanced toward the front of the bus, noticing many of the other passengers peering around the sides of their chairs and kneeling on their seat cushions, staring over the top of their backrests at the spectacle of eight naked passengers sitting side-by-side with our hands and fingers still embedded over our glistening genitals.

Suddenly, without warning, the driver swerved the bus into a roadside rest stop, squealing the tires next to a clump of trees and stomping down the aisle toward the eight of us with a crazed look on his face. At first I thought he was going to admonish us for our indecent behavior, or take a picture of us to report us to the police, but when I saw him unzipping his pants and pulling out his throbbing hard-on, I smiled.

"Have you got room for one more cock back here?" he said. "I need to get in on this action. This is the most exciting road trip I've had in ages..."

**8**

―――――

"**I** don't see why not," I smiled, nodding toward my friends. "It looks like you've got your pick of the litter back here. Does anything strike your fancy?"

The driver turned his head to appraise the eight of us lined up side-by-side on the bench seat, then his gaze suddenly stopped when he noticed the huge dripping cock resting between the legs of the pretty trans girl.

"Mmm," he said, licking his lips. "I wouldn't mind a piece of that..."

"Works for me," Samantha smiled, glancing up at the surprisingly young and cute driver. "But how exactly are we going to do this? We're already packed like sardines back here."

"Can I just *sit* on it?" the driver said. "I'm not usually into that kind of stuff, but you're incredibly hot and that thing is a piece of art..."

"Absolutely," Samantha nodded. "But how will you get off? You'll be facing the wrong way–"

"Let me take care of that," I smiled, standing up and turning around to face toward the front of the bus, rubbing my wet ass against the driver's bobbing pole. "While you're fucking him up the ass, he can pound my pussy. The rest of you are welcome to follow our lead if you want. I'm sure you're eager to try something a little more interesting than just giving each other another handie."

"Damn straight," Owen nodded, encouraging Lisa sitting next to him to mimic the driver's lead and sit on his pole.

After all the girls quickly followed suit and sat in each of the boy's laps, one-by-one, each of the other passengers on the bus slowly rose out of their seats, pulling their pants down in the middle of the aisle and pressing their hips against one another. Some were paired up boy/girl, some girl/girl, and some boy/boy, but it hardly seemed to matter. By this time, everyone was so turned on from watching the group of us getting our freak on at the back of the bus that they would have connected with just about anybody to get their rocks off at this point.

While a few of them thrust their dicks into their partner's willing backsides, some of them fucked their partner's pussies from behind, and some of them reached around the front of the person standing next to them to stimulate their partner manually. In the darkness of the dimmed cabin, it was hard to see who was pairing with whom, and that seemed to add to the excitement of the impromptu orgy. Whether it was a man or a woman, for many of the passengers, it was their first time joining with a same-sex partner, and certainly the first time they'd done anything so impulsive and risqué as fucking a complete stranger in the middle of the night on a lonely bus trip.

As the cabin began to fill with the sound of collective moans and groans, I had to smile as the bus driver's hips slammed against my ass while Samantha fucked him from behind. *The Chinese have an interesting proverb,* I thought to myself. *They say every problem is also an opportunity looking for a solution. I'll have to remember that at my upcoming business meeting later this morning...*

R eady for more erotic chills and thrills? Read the next volume in Jade's Erotic Adventures, *The Blind Girl*. Buy direct and save at victoriarusherotica. Or download from your favorite online bookstore here: retailer links.

*They say your other senses are heightened when one is compromised...*

# ALSO BY VICTORIA RUSH

## Adult Fairytales:

The Enchanted Forest: An Erotic Fairytale

The Land of Giants: An Erotic Fairytale

The Dragon's Lair: An Erotic Fairytale

Witch's Brew: An Erotic Fairytale

The Mage's Spell: An Erotic Fairytale

The Mermaid Lagoon: An Erotic Fairytale

The Coven: An Erotic Fairytale

Rapunzel: An Erotic Fairytale

The Seven Dwarfs: An Erotic Fairytale

The Land of Mutants: An Erotic Fairytale

The Erotic Temple: A Sexy Fairytale (Coming Soon)

**Erotica Themed Bundles:**

Voyeur: Lesbian Erotica Bundle

Public Affairs: A Lesbian Anthology

Futa Fantasies: The Ladyboy Collection

Threesomes: The Lesbian Collection

Threesomes - Volume 2: The Lesbian Collection

First Time: A Lesbian Anthology

Hedonism: An Erotic Anthology

Switch Hitters: Bisexual Erotica

Taboo Erotica: The Lesbian Series

BDSM: The Lesbian Collection

Party Games: The Erotic Collection

Party Games 2: The Erotic Collection

All Girl 1: Lesbian Erotica Bundle

All Girl 2: Lesbian Erotica Bundle

All Girl 3: Lesbian Erotica Bundle

All Girl 4: Lesbian Erotica Bundle

**Erotic Fairytale Bundles:**

Clover's Fantasy Adventures: Books 1 - 5

Clover's Fantasy Adventures: Books 6 - 10

**Erotic Fantasy:**

Pirate's Bounty: A Time Travel Adventure

Wild West: A Time Travel Adventure

Private Riley: A Time Travel Adventure

Cleopatra's Secret: A Time Travel Adventure

Bounty Hunter 2125: A Time Travel Adventure

Ninja Assassin: A Time Travel Adventure

The 300: A Time Travel Adventure

Arabian Nights: An Erotic Fairytale (coming soon...)

**Steamy Time Travel Bundles:**

Riley's Time Travel Adventures: Books 1 - 5

**Lesbian Erotica:**

The Dinner Party: Lesbian Voyeur Erotica

The Darkroom: Bisexual Voyeur Erotica

Naked Yoga: Lesbian Transgender Erotica

Nude Cruise: Bisexual Voyeur Erotica

Rush Hour: Taboo Public Sex

The Girl Next Door: First Time Lesbian Erotic Romance

Girls' Camp: Lesbian Group Sex

Wet Dream: Ladyboy Fantasy Erotica

The Convent: Taboo Sex with a Nun

Sex Robot: A Dream Sex Machine

The Personal Trainer: Getting Pumped at the Gym

The Dominatrix: BDSM Lesbian Domination

Webcam Chat: Lesbian Online Sex

Paint Me: A Kinky Bodypainting Workshop

The Toy Party: Girls Sharing Sex Toys

The Costume Party: Strapping One On

Swedish Sauna: Lesbian Group Sex

The Therapist: Taboo Lesbian Erotica

Elevator Shaft: Bisexual Threesomes Erotica

Ladyboy: Lesbian Transgender Erotica

Peep Show: Lesbian Voyeur Erotica

The Dare: Public Sex Erotica

Maid Service: Lesbian Threesomes Erotica

The Hitchhiker: First Time Lesbian Erotica

The Housesitter: Spycam Lesbian Erotica

The Spa: Lesbian Group Orgy

Parlor Games: Blindfold Sex Party

The Exchange Student: First Time Lesbian Erotica

The Hostel: Bisexual Group Erotica

The Harem: Lesbian Erotic Romance

The Orient Express: Lesbian Voyeur Erotica

The First Lady: A Forbidden Lesbian Erotic Romance

The Slave: Lesbian BDSM Erotica

The Masseuse: Lesbian Sensuous Erotica

Too Close for Comfort: Lesbian Forbidden Erotica

Naked Twister: A Wild Party Game

Lexi: The Sex App ( Lesbian Fantasy Erotica )

Call Girl: Lesbian Bisexual Threesomes Erotica

Circle Jill: Lesbian Masturbation Workshop

The Viewing Room: Masturbation Voyeur Erotica

Spin the Bottle: A Kinky Party Game

The Hair Salon: Lesbian Voyeur Erotica

Tribadism 1: Girls Only Sex Workshop

Tribadism 2: The Art of Scissoring

Tribadism 3: Threeway Hookups

The Kiss: A Game of Oral Sex

Pledge Week: Sorority Sisters

Carny Games 1: A Wild Sex Party

Carny Games 2: A Kinky Sex Party

Carny Games 3: An Erotic Sex Party

Dreamscape: An Artificial Reality Game

Glory Hole: Guess Who's On the Other Side

Joy Ride: A Late Night Erotic Bus Trip

The Blind Girl: An Erotic Romance(Coming Soon)

**Lesbian Erotica Bundles:**

Jade's Erotic Adventures: Books 1 - 5

Jade's Erotic Adventures: Books 6 - 10

Jade's Erotic Adventures: Books 11 - 15

Jade's Erotic Adventures: Books 16 - 20

Jade's Erotic Adventures: Books 21 - 25

Jade's Erotic Adventures: Books 26 - 30

Jade's Erotic Adventures: Books 31 - 35

Jade's Erotic Adventures: Books 36 - 40

Jade's Erotic Adventures: Books 41 - 45

Jade's Erotic Adventures: Books 46 - 50

Fifty Shades of Jade: Superbundle

**Standalone Stories:**

The Polynesian Girl: A Lesbian EroticRomance

# FOLLOW VICTORIA RUSH:

*Want to keep informed of my latest erotic book releases? Sign up for my newsletter and receive a FREE bonus book:*

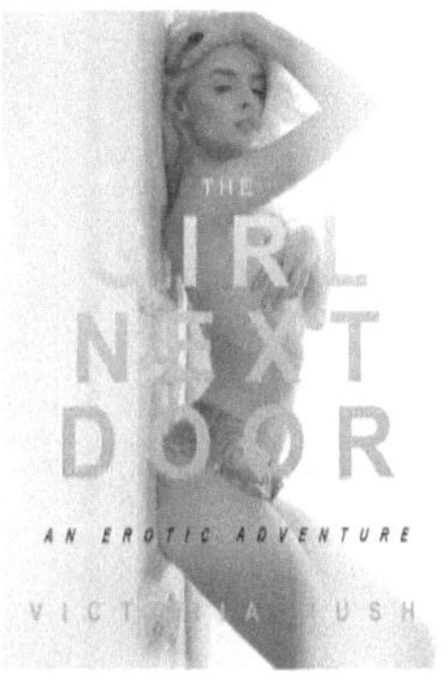

*Spying on the neighbors just got a lot more interesting...*